PETER RABB

EASTER ACTIVITY BOOK

CONTENTS

Peter Rabbit's Easter Eggs

Colouring eggs to give as presents has been an Easter custom for many years. Here Peter Rabbit shows you how to decorate special eggs.

Colourful Eggs

Peter Rabbit dyes his Easter eggs with vegetables from Mr. McGregor's garden.

1. Fill a saucepan with water, onion skins and a white egg. Ask an adult to boil the egg for half an hour.

2. When the water has cooled, sieve out the onion skins and add a few drops of vinegar to fix the colour.

3. Drain the hard-boiled egg with a slatted spoon and leave it to dry.

4. Rub vegetable oil on to the shell while it is still warm for a shiny finish.

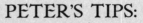

PETER'S TIPS:
You can also use beetroot, spinach, turmeric, tea and food colouring to dye Easter eggs.

Hollow Eggs

Give your lungs a work-out creating hollow eggs. You can thread these fragile eggs on a ribbon for an Easter garland.

1. Prick a hole with a darning needle in both ends of a room temperature egg. Chip away at the shell to make one hole bigger.

2. Break the egg yolk by poking it with the needle.

3. Blow through the small hole to drain the egg into a bowl. When the eggshell is empty, prop it in an egg cup and let it dry.

4. Carefully paint the egg and decorate it with stickers.

EGG DECORATIONS

After colouring your Easter eggs, varnish them with a coat of clear glue. Use anything from wool and ribbons, to sequins and stickers, for decorating Easter eggs.

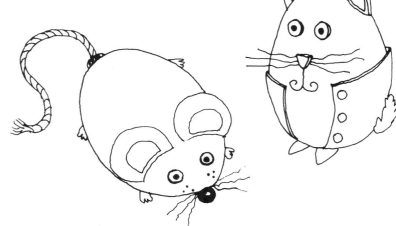

Egg Heads

To make a Peter Rabbit egg, cut out two rabbit ears from brown card and glue them to the back of the egg. Paint on Peter's face and blue jacket, then glue a cotton ball to the back of the egg for a tail. What other animals you can make?

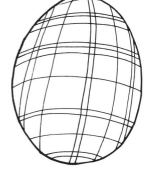

Wax Designs

Colour a warm hard-boiled egg with a crayon. The egg's heat will melt the wax and give the eggshell a shiny coating. When the egg has cooled, scratch a design into the wax using a darning needle. For the reverse effect, crayon a pattern on the egg before dyeing it. The dye will not take to the wax.

Tape Creations

Wind masking tape around a hard-boiled egg in a pattern, such as stripes or criss-cross. Paint the uncovered parts of the eggshell and remove the tape when the paint has dried.

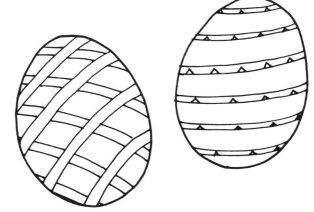

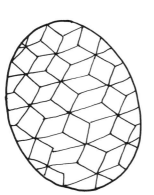

Pretty Patterns

Wrap an egg in a piece of scrap fabric, then place it in the foot of an old sheer stocking. Boil the egg and the cloth's pattern will transfer to the eggshell. Try using flowers and leaves instead of fabric.

JEMIMA'S EGG HUNT

Silly Jemima Puddle-duck has hidden her eggs in the foxy
gentleman's shed. Trace a path through the feathery maze
to Jemima's nest. Then find ten eggs hidden in the maze
and place a sticker over each one.

START

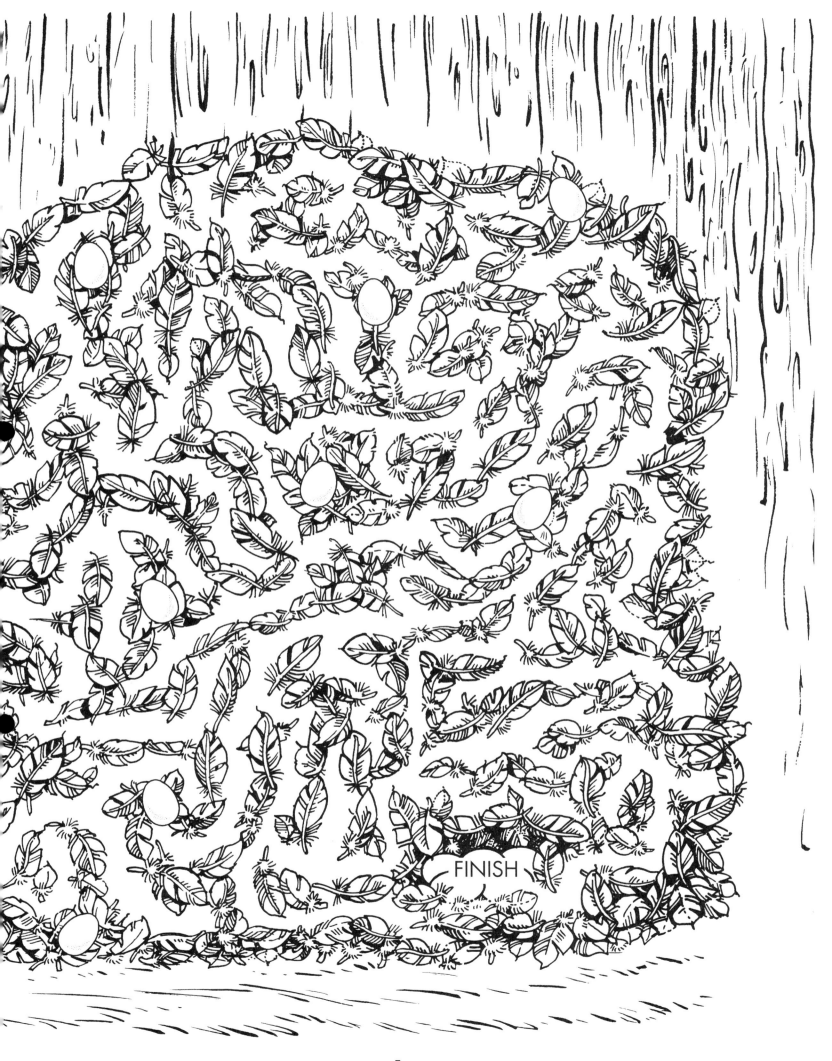

FINISH

EASTER TREE

A traditional Easter tree makes a beautiful centrepiece.
Display your hollow eggs on the tree's branches and make
decorations featuring Peter Rabbit and his friends.

1. Find a well-shaped tree branch with many twigs.
Paint it white or silver and leave it to dry.

2. Paint a springtime design, such as
flowers, Easter eggs or Peter Rabbit,
on a flowerpot. When it is dry, fill the
flowerpot with damp sand or soil and
firmly plant the branch.

3. Decorate the branch with colourful
hollow eggs or sweets. Stick Easter
stickers on coloured card, cut them
out, then make a hole at the top of each
sticker. Thread a ribbon through each hole
and hang the decorations from twigs.

PETER'S TIPS:
• To hang a hollow egg from an Easter tree, tie
a thread around a used matchstick and push it
inside the egg's large hole. Jiggle the thread
until the matchstick hangs horizontally and cannot
come out of the egg, then tie the thread to a twig.

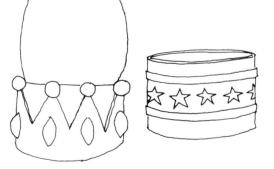

EGG CUPS

Serve coloured, hard-boiled eggs in
home-made egg cups for Easter breakfast,
or use them to display special Easter eggs.

1. Cut a toilet roll tube widthways
into three rings.

2. Paint the rings or glue a band of
coloured paper, wrapping paper or
kitchen foil around them.

3. Decorate the rings any way you
like. Stick on small stickers, or glue
on sequins, glitter, dried flowers,
beads or trimming.

4. Place an egg in each cup.

EASTER BASKET

Weave a basket to hold your Easter eggs, or leave it empty for the Easter Bunny to fill with sweets.

1. Cut out 12 strips of coloured card, each measuring 38 x 2.5 cm (15 x 1 inch). Make two pencil marks on each strip, 11 cm (4¼ inches) from both ends.

2. Cut out three long strips, each measuring 64 x 2.5 cm (25½ x 1 inch), from a different colour of card.

3. Lay six of the short strips beside each other and stick down the top ends with masking tape.

4. Weave in each of the remaining six short strips, passing them under and over through the taped-down strips, between the pencil marks.

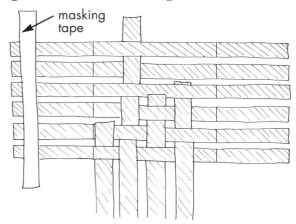

masking tape

5. Carefully remove the masking tape and bend the ends of all the strips upwards at the pencil marks.

6. Weave a long strip through all four sides of the basket. Carefully bend the strip around the corners. Tuck the ends inside the basket and glue them in place.

7. Weave the two remaining long strips in the same way to build up the basket.

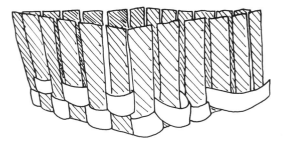

8. Fold the top ends alternately inside and outside the basket. Glue the ends in place to create a neat edge of one colour.

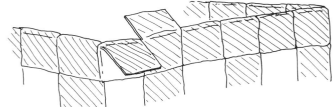

9. Cut out a strip of card 40 x 2.5 cm (16 x 1 inch) long. Glue this handle inside the basket.

BEATRIX POTTER'S EGG ROLL

Every Easter, Beatrix Potter would decorate Easter eggs for the children in her Lake District village.
The children would roll their Easter eggs down a hill, and those whose eggs did not crack were the winners.
Why not have an egg roll with your friends this Easter?

Easter eggs painted by Beatrix Potter for local children known as the "Pace Eggers".

EGG PUZZLE

Can you find the right stickers to make these cracked eggs whole again? Then colour in the black-and-white halves to match the stickers.

EASTER RECIPES

Chocolate eggs are not the only special foods to enjoy at Easter! These tasty recipes are simple to make, but ask an adult for help cutting and handling hot objects. Remember, good cooks always clean up the kitchen when they have finished.

JEMIMA'S CHOCOLATE NESTS

These chocolate treats are quick and easy to make. Try giving them as place settings for Easter dinner or as scrumptious party favours!

Ingredients:

- 50 g (1¾ oz) butter
- 2 tbsp golden syrup
- 4 tbsp cocoa powder
- 7 heaped tbsp cornflakes
- 7 heaped tbsp rice cereal
- small, sugar-coated chocolate eggs
- 12 cupcake cases

Method

1. With an adult's help, melt the butter and golden syrup together in a saucepan over low heat.

2. Add in the cocoa powder and stir well to remove any lumps.

3. Mix in both cereals, blending well to coat the cereal in chocolate.

4. Drop a spoonful of the mixture into each cupcake case. To form the nests, press a hollow in the middle of each with your thumb.

5. Refrigerate the nests until they set, then fill them with small, sugar-coated chocolate eggs.

PETER'S TIPS:
For variety, try adding raisins, chopped nuts or your favourite cereal to the chocolate mixture.

BISCUIT BONNETS

Great fun to assemble at an Easter party, these snacks do not require any cooking.

Ingredients:

- 6 round cookies
- 6 marshmallows   • ready-made icing
- selection of small sweets, sugar flowers and dried fruits

Method

1. Spread a teaspoon of icing thickly on to each cookie.

2. Stick a marshmallow on to the icing to make hats.

3. Decorate around the brim of each hat with tiny sweets or fruits, sticking them to the icing.

FLOPSY'S BERRY BASKETS

You can eat these tasty baskets whole, not just the berries inside!

Ingredients:

- packet of instant dessert mix and milk
- flat-bottomed ice cream cones
- thick, red licorice
- 50 g (1¾ oz) desiccated coconut
- berries or berry sweets
- green food colouring

Method

1. Following the directions on the package, whisk the instant dessert mix and milk together in a bowl then refrigerate to chill.

2. Spoon the dessert mixture into the ice cream cones. One package of dessert mix should fill about five or six cones.

3. Mix the desiccated coconut with a few drops of green food colouring. Sprinkle a spoonful of green coconut on top of each cone.

4. Decorate each basket with a few berries and make handles from strips of red licorice. Serve immediately, before the baskets become soggy.

Mrs. Rabbit's Hot Cross Buns

Traditionally baked on Good Friday, sweet hot cross buns taste delicious warm from the oven or toasted and spread with butter.

Ingredients:

- 1 tbsp dried yeast
- 250 ml (1/2 pint) milk
- 60 g (2 oz) sugar, plus 2 tbsp for glaze
- 450 g (16 oz) plain flour
- 50 g (1 3/4 oz) butter
- 1 tsp salt
- 2 tbsp water
- 100 g (3 1/2 oz) mixed dried fruit
- 2 tsp mixed spice

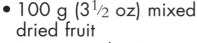

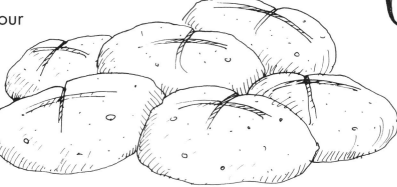

Method

1. With an adult's help, heat the milk in a saucepan until just warm, then mix in the yeast and 1 tsp of sugar. Leave the mixture in a warm place for 20 minutes until frothy.

2. Preheat the oven to 200°C (400°F). Combine the flour and salt in a large mixing bowl, then rub the butter into the mixture with your fingertips.

3. Add the rest of the sugar, the mixed spice and the mixed dried fruit to the flour mixture and blend well.

4. Stir in the yeast mixture, then knead the dough on a floured surface for about five minutes. (Kneading means pressing and stretching the dough with your hands.)

5. Shape the dough into a ball, then put it back in the mixing bowl. Cover the bowl with a clean cloth and leave it in a warm place for 45 minutes, until the dough doubles in size.

6. Divide the dough and pat it into 12 buns. Place them on a greased baking tray and have an adult make a cross on each bun with a sharp knife. Bake the buns in the oven for 15-20 minutes, until risen and golden brown.

7. Mix two tablespoons of sugar with two tablespoons of boiled water until the sugar dissolves. Brush this glaze on the buns while they are still hot.

PETER'S TIPS:
Keep the dough away from draughts, or else it will not rise.

BABY ANIMALS

Playful baby animals are a cheery sign of springtime. Can you match each group of baby animals with a sticker of their mother?

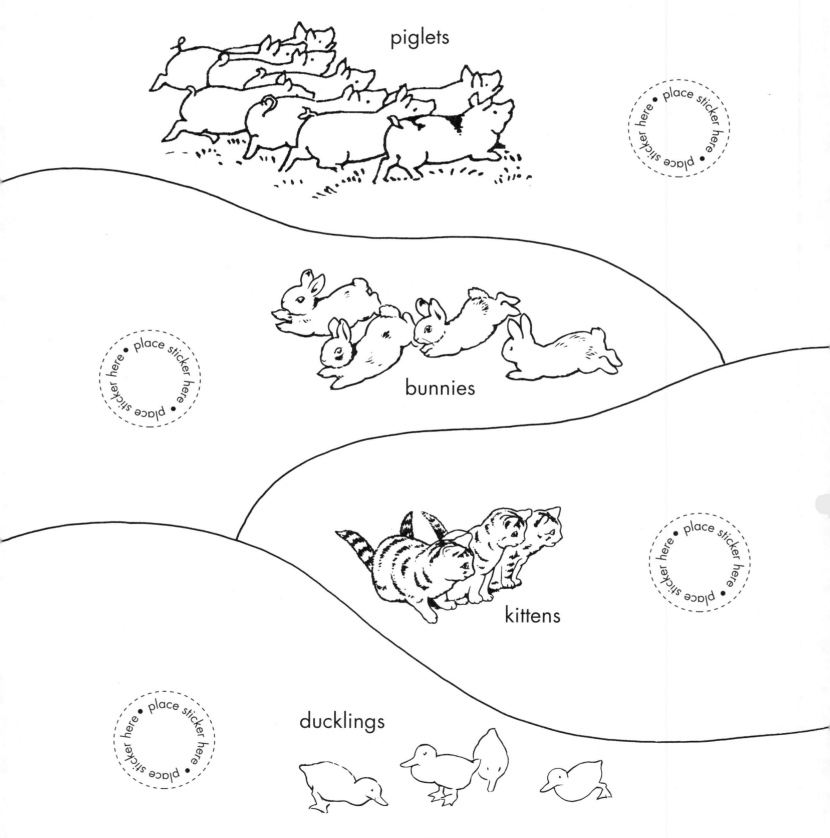

piglets

place sticker here

place sticker here

bunnies

kittens

place sticker here

ducklings

place sticker here

Jemima's Egg Hunt, *pages 4–5*

Spot the Difference, *page 16*

Hat Jumble, *page 15*

Egg Puzzle, *page 8*

Baby Animals, *page 12*

Rebus Letter, *page 20*

Extra stickers for decorating Easter eggs, Easter tree and cards

Dot~to~Dot

Who is eating radishes in Mr. McGregor's garden?
Join up the dots to find out, then colour in the picture.

EASTER BONNET

People wear their finest clothes and smart, new hats to celebrate Easter. Here Jemima Puddle-duck explains how to create a bonnet just like the one that she wears. Why not stage an Easter parade and model your bonnet?

1. Draw a big semicircle on a large piece of card.

2. Mark the bonnet template on your semicircle, as shown. Cut out the shape, remembering to cut between B and C. Cut a slit on either side of the semicircle.

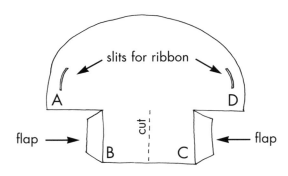

3. Fold along the dotted lines. Then overlap B and C slightly and glue them in place to form the back of the bonnet.

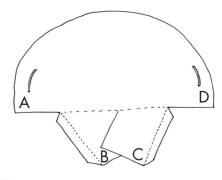

4. Bend the semicircle and glue A to B and C to D using the flaps. Glue the flaps inside the bonnet rather than outside, as shown.

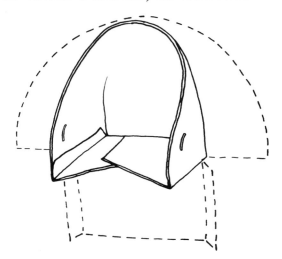

5. Thread a wide ribbon through one slit, over the top of the bonnet and through the other slit. Glue crêpe paper frills along the back and sides of the bonnet. Now you are ready for the Easter parade!

PETER'S TIPS:
• To make an easy Easter bonnet, attach a length of ribbon to either side of a paper plate. Decorate the plate with anything from scrunched up tissue paper, feathers and fabric, to paper daffodils and pompom chicks.

14

HAT JUMBLE

Can you help Tom Kitten, Jemima Puddle-duck,
Mrs. Tiggy-winkle and Benjamin Bunny to find their hats?
Follow each line to see where it leads, then place a sticker
of the hat's owner at the end.

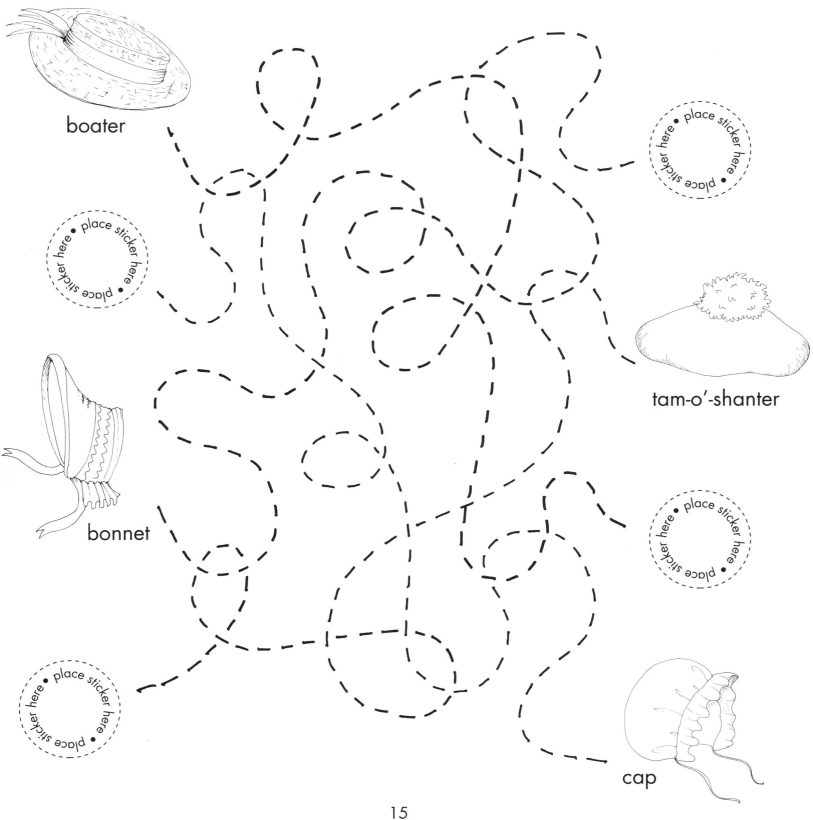

boater

place sticker here • place sticker here

place sticker here • place sticker here

tam-o'-shanter

bonnet

place sticker here • place sticker here

place sticker here • place sticker here

cap

15

SPOT THE DIFFERENCE

There are six differences between these two pictures.
Spot the missing objects and replace them with stickers.

GARDEN CROSSWORD

Across

2. Peter Rabbit squeezes under the garden _ _ _ _. (4)

4. Object used to water flowers and plants. (11)

5. Leafy green vegetable that rabbits like to nibble. (7)

6. Crunchy red vegetable, eaten by Peter Rabbit. (6)

8. Clay container for growing flowers. (9)

Down

1. Insect with feelers and brightly coloured wings. (9)

3. Wears old clothes and frightens birds away from crops. (9)

4. Has one wheel and two handles and is used to carry loads. (11)

7. Small tool for planting seeds. (6)

9. Strong-smelling vegetable that can make you cry. (5)

POMPOM CHICK

Cheep! Cheep! Cheep! Sally Henny Penny is very proud of her fluffy, yellow brood. Here you can make a woolly pompom chick of your own.

1. Using compasses, draw two circles on stiff card, each measuring 9 cm (3½ inches) across. Then draw a smaller circle 3 cm (1 inch) wide inside each big circle. Cut out the circles, both inner and outer, to make rings.

2. Stack one ring on top of the other and wind yellow wool around them until they are thickly covered and the hole in the centre gets smaller. Use several lengths of wool instead of one long piece.

3. Cut through the wool, between the two rings. Slip a piece of wool between the rings. Tie it tightly, then slide off the rings.

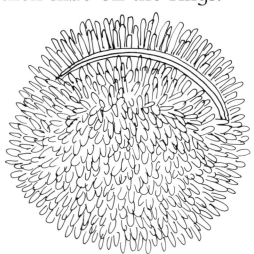

4. Make a smaller pompom in the same way, using rings 6 cm (2½ inches) across with centres 2 cm (³/4 inch) wide. Glue the smaller pompom on top of the larger pompom for the chick's head.

5. Draw the chick's feet on orange felt. Cut out the feet and glue them to the bottom of the chick. Cut out a small diamond of orange felt, bend it in half and glue it to the head for a beak. Glue on two tiny circles of black felt for eyes.

PETER'S TIPS:
• If you don't have compasses, tie a piece of string to a pencil. Hold the end of the string taut and arc the pencil round to draw a circle.

• Try making a furry Peter Rabbit from brown wool or a fuzzy Tom Kitten from grey wool.

SPRING CRAFTS

Nature springs to life just in time for Easter. You can grow cress, delicious in salads, in a bunny planter. For greenery that lasts well past Easter, make a bouquet of paper daffodils.

BUNNY PLANTER

1. Cut off one side of a pint-sized milk carton, then paint the carton brown.

2. Cut out two rabbit ears from card and paint them brown. When the ears are dry, cut out two smaller ear shapes from pink felt and glue them to the middle of the ears.

3. Glue the ears to the front corners of the carton. Stick a cotton ball on to the back to make a fluffy tail.

4. Glue on two small, black buttons for the rabbit's eyes, add a triangle of pink felt for a nose and draw whiskers with a black marker pen.

5. Fill the planter with soil and sow a packet of cress seeds. Keep the soil moist, and soon your bunny will grow a thick coat of cress.

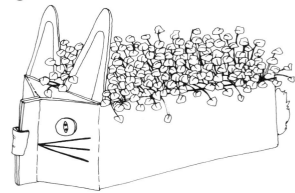

PAPER DAFFODIL

1. Draw a daffodil shape with six petals on to a piece of card. Cut out the daffodil shape and paint it yellow.

2. Cut out an egg cup from an egg carton and paint it yellow. When the paint has dried, glue the base of the egg cup to the flower's centre.

3. Using the tip of a pencil, poke a tiny hole in the centre of the flower, piercing through both the card and the egg cup.

4. To make a stem, push a long, green pipe cleaner or flexible straw through the hole and bend the end.

REBUS LETTER

To read the letter, fill in the missing words by placing the correct stickers over the dotted shapes.

Dear Cousin Benjamin,

I am writing to tell you of my recent adventures

in Mr. McGregor's garden. First, I squeezed under

the [ ]. Then I ate some [ ], French beans,

and some [ ]. Imagine my fright when Mr. McGregor

caught sight of me and chased after me with a [ ].

As I ran away, I lost my [ ] and caught the buttons

on my new [ ] on a gooseberry net.

Mr. McGregor has used my clothes for a [ ] to

frighten the [ ]. Will you kindly help me get them back?

Your affectionate cousin,

Peter Rabbit

EASTER CARDS

Would you like to wish somebody special a happy Easter?
Colour in these cards and cut them out. Write a message inside,
then deliver Easter greetings to your family and friends.

HAPPY EASTER

BEST WISHES

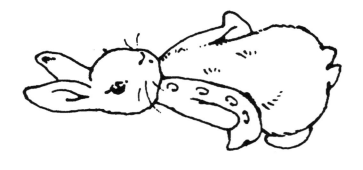

Carefully cut along the wing line on the bottom chick. When you have cut out and folded the card, bend the wing backwards to reveal the message inside.

HAPPY EASTER